WINSTON

WRITTEN BY
Pamela Duncan Edwards

ILLUSTRATED BY
Benji Davies

WAS WORRIED

Winston had a splinter in his paw.

"OH NO!" wailed Winston.

"There's nothing as bad as having a splinter in your paw."

"I'm so unfortunate. Everything always happens to me."

"Hi Winston," barked Angus.
"Want to bite some bicycle tyres?"

"I can't," cried Winston. "I need to see the vet.
I've got a splinter in my paw."

"Gosh!" said Angus. "Is it a big splinter?"
"It is!" said Winston proudly.

THUNK!

It's a
great BIG
splinter.

"Nothing is as bad as having a splinter in your paw."

"I'm so unfortunate."

"Everything always happens to me."

"Hey Winston," barked Rex.
"How about sniffing around the dustbins?"

"I can't," cried Winston. "I need to see the vet.
I've got a splinter in my paw."

"Wow!" said Rex.
"Is it a big splinter?"

"It is!"
said Winston
proudly.

It's a great
BIG, HUGE
splinter.

"Nothing is as bad as having a splinter in your paw."

"I'm so unfortunate. Everything always happens to me."

"Winston!" barked Bert.
"I've found a new flower bed. Let's dig!"

"I can't," cried Winston.
"I need to see the vet.
I've got a splinter in my paw."

"Nothing is as bad as having a splinter in your paw."

"I'm so unfortunate. Everything always happens to me."

"Hello Winston," barked Sophie.
"Shall we go and chase some cats?"

"I can't," cried Winston. "I need to see the vet.
I've got a splinter in my paw."

"Everything always happens to me."

Winston sucked his sore paw.

But something felt different . . .

"Where's my splinter?"
cried Winston.

"It's disappeared!"

Winston gave his paw a big, wet lick.

"Oh no!" yelped Winston.
"I need to see the vet.
I've got a wobbly loose tooth."

"Nothing is as bad as having a wobbly loose tooth."

"Why does everything always happen to me?"